I Love You ACROSS THE WORLD

Written by
Kim Bushman Aguilar

Illustrated by
Jenni Feidler-Aguilar

To the toddler version of my teenage son—I would have delightedly read this to you when you were little, as I did so many others. I hope your love of reading lasts a lifetime. I love you across the world, Clark, and all the way back home again.
~ Kim

For Natalie and Camila, I love you with all my corazon! Love, Mom
~ Jenni Feidler-Aguilar

This edition first published in 2022
by Lawley Publishing,
a division of Lawley Enterprises LLC.

Lawley Publishing
70 S. Val Vista Dr. #A3 #188
Gilbert, AZ 85296
www.LawleyPublishing.com

North, South, East, West–
You're the one that I love best!

I love you in
Germany,

German:
ich liebe dich

I love you in
Japan.

Japanese:
watashi wa

I love you in
Korea,
Korean:
salanghae

I love you in
Iran!
Persian:
doostetaan daaram

I love you in
Finland,
Holland,
and Russia,

Finnish:
Minä rakastan sinua

Dutch:
ik hou van je

Russian:
ya tebya lyublyu

There's no place on earth
I wouldn't want to see ya!

I love you in
Brazil,

Portuguese:
eu te amo

I love you in
Tibet.

Tibetan:
nga rang la ga khi

I love you in places
I haven't even been yet!

I love you in
Iceland,

Icelandic:
é elska Þig

I love you in
Belgium.
Flemish:
Ik zie je graag
If I take a trip,
you're always welcome!

I love you in
Mexico,
Fiji,
Botswana,

Spanish:
te quiero

iTaukei:
au lomani iko

Setswana:
ke a go rata

Packing's
a cinch.

There's really
no drama!

I love you in Morocco,

Moroccan Arabic:
kan Hha abek

I love you in
Mali.

Bambara:
m'bi fe

I love you in
Sri Lanka,

Sinhala:
mama oyāta ādareyi

I love you in
Bali!

Balinese:
titiyang tresna sareng ragane

I love you in China,

Mandarin: wǒ ài nǐ

I love you in Peru.
Spanish: te amo
One thing you should know, my love is true blue!

I love you in Italy,
and Greece, and France,

Italian:
ti amo

Greek:
se agapó

French:
je t'aime

You know what
they say chérie–

Life
is a
dance!

I love you in
Israel,

Hebrew:
ani ohev otakh

I love you in
India.

Hindi:
main tumhen pyaar kara taa huun

I love you in
Denmark,

Danish:
jeg elsker dig

I love you in
Romania!
Romanian:
te iubesc

And no matter how far we roam,
Or even if we stay close to home–

I love you
across the world.

Kim Bushman Aguilar wrote ***I Love You Across the World*** while daydreaming about all the places she's been and all the places she has yet to see. Some of her favorite memories include: packing a lunch to the top of the Eiffel Tower, breathing the fragrant air of the Keukenhof tulip gardens, sailing down the Nile River among the temples of kings and queens, listening to Mozart's Eine kleine Nachtmusik in the fortress above Salzburg, swimming with the stars and eating lobster spaghetti in Greece, pushing the family van back onto the ferry after it broke down in Morocco, climbing The Pyramid of the Sun in Teotihuancan with her husband and son, and living in Germany with floor to ceiling golden views of the Rhine. She is the author of five books for children: ***The Bushmans Come to America, The Bushmans in Nauvoo, Use Your Words, I Love You Across the World,*** and the forthcoming ***Tell Everyone***. Please visit **kimbushmanaguilar.com** for further tidbits about her life and work.

Jenni Feidler-Aguilar is an artist, art teacher, mom, wife, and a life-long dreamer. She has always believed that when you put your mind to it, you can achieve your dreams. An Arizona native, Jenni lived one of her first dreams when she moved to Florence, Italy, to study art. Following her wanderlust, she completed her student teaching in Managua, Nicaragua, where she met her husband and stayed a few more years. Having traveled to many other countries during this time, Jenni learned just how incredible our world is. She continues to love learning about other cultures and experiencing life from other perspectives. Jenni now lives back in Arizona with her husband and two beautiful daughters, where she is an Art Teacher. She is also a practicing artist, completing both private and public pieces such as murals, chalk art festival pieces, and a fiberglass bench in Downtown Gilbert. If you asked Jenni what she wants to be when she grows up, she wouldn't give you one answer because she has many dreams yet to achieve. Yet "children's book illustrator" is at the top of her list, proving that dreams do, indeed, come true.

CPSIA information can be obtained
at www.ICGtesting.com
Printed in the USA
BVRC100943030222
627976BV00008B/248

* 9 7 8 1 9 5 6 3 5 7 0 8 0 *